DOG DID iT!

by Lynne Garner
Illustrated by Mike Brownlow

PICCADILLY PRESS • LONDON

Boris loved to eat
green worm porridge.

It was just SO nice!

Boris loved to eat it even though . . .

green worm porridge upset his belly.

One day, Boris had lots of huge helpings of
green worm porridge for breakfast.

Later, on the way to the bus stop,

he felt his belly grumble and growl.

It growled and rumbled.

It rumbled and grumbled.

Boris held his belly.

"Oh no!" he said quietly.

But it was too late!

"What a pong!
Who did a trouser trumpet?"
asked an old troll, wiping her nose.

"Oh, how rude! Who trottered?" asked her friend.

Boris pretended it wasn't him.

"Mummy, someone was naughty and did a tooter," said a little troll who was covered in mud.

Everyone looked at Boris and Boris looked around.

Boris looked at Dog and Dog looked at Boris.

"Sorry Dog," said Boris quietly, so only Dog could hear.

Then Boris pointed at Dog and Dog looked sad.

"Dog did it!" said Boris.

When Boris was walking
through town,
he felt his belly gurgle
and babble.
It babbled and curdled.
It curdled and gurgled.

Boris looked around as he held his belly.

"Oh no!" said Boris to himself.

But he couldn't stop it.

"Who did that smelly blampf?" asked a little troll picking his nose. "It's putting me right off my food."

"Oh, what a whiffy blurt, who did that?" asked his sister.

Boris pretended it wasn't him.

"That IS an awful pong, who just blurped?"
asked a troll burying his nose in his armpit.

Everyone looked at Boris and Boris

looked around.

Boris looked at Dog and Dog looked at Boris.
"Sorry Dog," said Boris quietly, so only Dog could hear.

Then Boris pointed at
Dog and Dog looked sad.

"Dog did it!" said Boris.

Boris went to the park to feed the ducks.

Dog ate most of the bread when Boris wasn't looking.
It was just SO nice, even though
it did upset his belly.

Dog felt his belly gurgle and bubble.
It bubbled and burbled. It burbled and gurgled.

"Who did that flappy whoof?"
asked a troll scrunching up his nose.

"That's awful! Who did that flutterblast?"
asked a big gruff troll.

Boris looked around because he *knew* it wasn't him.

"That's horrid! Who did that flabbergaster?"
asked a small troll burying her nose in her
crunchy bug sandwich.

Everyone looked at Boris and
Boris looked for Dog.

But Dog had run away . . .

Everyone

pointed at Boris.

"YOU did it!" they said.

"But dog really DID do it,"
Boris said crossly, as
he walked off.

And that's not all Dog did!